Unidentified Love

Kyros Amphiptere and Orion T. Hunter

The authors wish to thank their friends and families who put up with them constantly talking about, and often to, imaginary people.

Find more of the authors' short stories, as well as what inspired this story, on the authors' blog at: http://www.thirdwar.net/blog/

Chapter One

"I didn't mean to fall for you, it just happened," I told him while we sat together in the bed of his truck under the crescent moon.

Nick looked at me, those big, brown eyes wet with unshed tears. "I can't. I like you, but..." His words tapered off as he looked down at his feet. He mumbled out some more words, but I couldn't hear him.

I wanted so desperately to reach out and touch him, comfort him somehow, but fear kept me on my side of the truck.

"I can't hear you when you mumble into your overalls like that. Look at me, please." *He's so upset he can't even look at me. I shouldn't have said anything. Just forget it. Let's go back to being friends. Please, please, please.*

"I said, 'Why did you have to tell me you liked me like that?' I'm not..." He paused, looking everywhere but at me. "I don't...."

"I know, you don't feel that way about me. Forget I said anything." My face was practically on fire with embarrassment.

"Ben, stop. Just stop!" Nick shouted.

Now *I* was the one close to tears.

Nick reached out and took my hand. "I do have feelings for you, but my dad.... He's a general at the base. He expects me to join the military and follow in his footsteps. I can't do that if I'm with you. They kick people

1

like us out. My dad told me a story once about a guy they thought was gay in their platoon. They beat him up so bad that he wasn't able to walk ever again." He hopped out of the pickup and paced back and forth between the edge of the cornfield and his truck. "He *laughed* when he told me that story. He helped break a man's spine so he'd never walk again and he bragged about it, like it was one of those damn medals on his chest. What do you think he'd do to me – or to you, for that matter, if he found out. I can't take that kind of chance."

My hearts had been doing the Snoopy Happy Dance ever since Nick admitted that he had feelings for me too. I knew he was right, I should be worried about his father's reaction, but I couldn't think about that. All I could think about was that Nick liked me.

"Ben!" Nick snapped his fingers in front of my face. "Earth to Ben." He chuckled at me. "I swear, sometimes it's like your brain is in outer space."

I couldn't resist a laugh of my own. *If you only knew how true that was.* "You'd like that, wouldn't you. You've been fascinated by all things extraterrestrial ever since we saw ET when it came out a few months ago."

"Just you wait. One day, I'll prove that ETs are real." Nick placed his hand over his heart. "It's my destiny, I just know it."

"Maybe you're right. Maybe one day you will discover that ETs have been visiting Earth for a long time."

"Don't laugh at me. I'm going to do it," Nick said,

puffing out his chest.

"I'm not laughing at you. It's one of the things that made me fall for you. I think it's cute."

Nick smiled up at me.

I jumped down beside my friend and pulled him into a hug. When I drew back, Nick had this strange look in his eyes.

"What?"

The only response I got was Nick dragging me deep into the head-height corn field.

Afterwards, we lay spent, lost in thought.

I broke the silence. "That was amazing. I thought it would be good, but, wow."

Nick smiled at me. "That was...incredible." But the smile faded and Nick's face turned grim. "Ben, this can't happen. It's nice to dream, but... It. Can. Never. Happen. Again. We can't be together like that."

"Maybe not now, but someday. Maybe someday things will change and we can be together," I offered.

Nick shook his head. "I don't think that will ever happen. If it does, well, then maybe...."

"If it does," I said, "then I'll be right here waiting for you."

The watch on Nick's wrist beeped. "Ah shit. Dad's going to be home soon. I have to go." He stood, hastily making his clothes presentable.

"Are you sure you can't stay just a little longer?" I asked. "We could...."

Nick shook his head. "I can't. If I'm not home when dad gets there, he'll get pissed and be shitty to me all evening."

I adjusted my clothes as we walked back to his truck.

The truck's engine roared to life.

Leaning through the open window, I couldn't resist giving him a kiss goodbye.

Several long moments passed before he broke the kiss. "I gotta go. I'm late already."

I smiled. "Ok, but if you change your mind, you know where to find me." I gestured with my head toward the farmhouse on the other side of the cornfield.

"I know. See you later, Ben," Nick shouted as his truck pulled away.

He was barely out of sight when *my* watch beeped.

I raised my wrist to my mouth. "Yes, Mother. You can beam me up now."

A soft glow surrounded me as I was transported to the waiting shuttle.

I'd just materialized when she started lecturing me. "You shouldn't get involved with a human," she said, stabbing a finger at me. "He's just going to break your hearts. You know how they are, humans are too fickle. They fall in and out of love whenever the wind changes direction. They don't mate for life like our people."

Ben sighed. "Nick's different, Mom. You'll see."

His mother shook her head and rolled her eyes.

Glancing at the monitor over her shoulder, I watched

4

Nick's truck do an abrupt u-turn and start heading back to where we'd parted.

"Looks like you were wrong, Mom. Nick does love me. Beam me back down there."

Chapter Two

The phone nearly vibrated off the bedside table before Nick blindly grabbed and pulled it under the covers to his ear. Groggily he spat out, "General Pearson. You just woke me up, so this had better be good."

A high-pitched female voice answered. "Mr. Pearson? This is Jenny from Forever Flowers. I'm afraid we have a problem with the flowers you ordered. Could you come down to our shop as soon as possible?"

Fully awake now, Nick sat up in bed, knocking the covers off both him and Ben.

"Hey, what's the big idea? I was asleep over here," Ben whined.

"Well, you have to get up. That was the florist. Some problem with the flowers for our wedding."

They arrived in the middle of a tornado of activity. People were rushing in every direction.

Grabbing a young woman flying by, Nick barked, "Excuse me. We received a call from you...."

The woman's face went scarlet in a moment.

"You must be Mr. Pearson. I'm Jenny, the one who called you. We got in this morning to finish up the flowers for your wedding and discovered that something knocked down the power lines last night. All our flowers were in the refrigerator, but with the power out and how hot it was last night, they've all wilted beyond recovery. I've made calls to every other florist in the area, but they were all hit by the outage too. I'm so sorry."

The poor girl was in tears by the time she finished.

Ben stepped in and hugged her, cutting off the sharp comment Nick had been about to make.

"It's okay. We know it's not your fault," Ben said, consoling her. "I'm sure it was just a freak accident that power went out to all the areas with flower shops." A weird, faraway look came over his face, then he sighed heavily. "We don't really need a lot of flowers, just something for our lapels." Looking around the shop, he spotted some flowers on the windowsill. "What about those?"

Her eyebrows rose. "The daisies? They're from the yard next door. I brought them in to cheer up the place. Besides, they're too common for a wedding, don't you think?"

Nick smiled for the first time since they'd arrived at the shop. "Not for our wedding. They were the first flowers Ben ever gave me, back when we first started dating." He chuckled. "I suspect he picked them from my side yard."

"I did, actually. I just liked how bright they were. They reminded me of you. Isn't it the thought that counts?"

Nick bent down to kiss Ben. "Yes, it is. We'll take them."

The florist packaged the delicate flowers and they left for the venue.

The guests had already begun arriving by the time Nick and Ben got to the country club. The first thing Nick saw when they walked through the doors were his parents.

His dad stood rigid, disapproval radiating from every pore of his lean, uniform-clad body. His mother waved and smiled at him until his dad fixed her with a sour look and she lowered her hand timidly.

Rolling his eyes, Nick asked Ben, "Did you ever hear back from your mother? Is she joining us today?"

Ben was about to answer when a sultry voice from over his shoulder answered, "Of course, dear. I wouldn't miss it for this or any other world."

They both turned to find Ben's model-perfect mother standing just inside the door, dressed in a decidedly high fashion, low cut dress with a huge hat. Both in black.

Ben put his hand over his face.

"Mom, you don't wear *black* to a wedding. Especially not mine."

"I'm truly sorry, dear. It was all I had with me when you sprang this news on me."

"I didn't spring it on you. I've called and left messages for months now. You could have picked something up on your way here, you know."

"There wasn't time, darling. I just got in a little bit ago."

The justice of the peace cleared his throat from the doorway to the banquet room behind them. "We're ready to get this started whenever you are, gentlemen." He then offered his arm to Ben's mother and led the parents to their seats.

Nick looked at Ben. "Are you ready to do this? To be my husband?"

Ben smiled at him, melting his insides like he had since they were teenagers.

"I've waited for this day for years. Let's do it."

Right at that moment, Nick's cell phone went off in his pocket, earning him a severe look from Ben.

"Don't you *dare* answer that. It's our wedding day. The base can be carried off by little green men, for all I care. Today is for us."

Nick had already slid his finger across the display to answer the phone so he shrugged, giving Ben a 'sorry' grin as he brought the device to his ear.

"Pearson here."

"Sir, we've been trying to reach you. One half hour ago, we detected a UFO in the area near Groom Lake. It paused briefly, then disappeared from the radar."

Beside him, Ben whispered, "Let Miles handle whatever it is. We have guests waiting for us."

Lowering the phone to his side, Nick hissed, "It's important. We have a UFO sighting nearby. I need to get back to the base."

Ben's eyes went cold. "Oh. So it's more important than our wedding? Is that what you're saying?"

Nick let out an exasperated sigh. "No, but couldn't we postpone it for one day. I'm sure our guests would understand."

9

"Really? You think so, huh? Okay, fine. You go in and explain to all our guests, including your parents and *my* mother, how your job is more important than our relationship."

Nick winced. "C'mon, don't be that way. You know how long I've been looking for proof that aliens exist. I can't leave this up to anyone else. Not even Miles."

"If you leave, there won't be a wedding. Ever!" Ben said, crossing his arms across his chest, the ultimatum stamped upon his face.

Nick took a sharp breath. "After everything we've gone through to be together? After the years we waited for it to be legal and for the military to allow me to marry another man? You can't be serious."

"Try me and find out."

Nick realized the phone was still in his hand and that his second-in-command had heard the entire exchange. Raising it back to his ear, he cleared his throat, then said, "Miles, I'm at my wedding. I'm marrying the love of my life today. You'll have to handle this one without me."

Miles chuckled across the phone line. "Looks like I win the bet with Parker then. He was sure you'd drop everything and head back here. I told him he didn't know Ben well enough if he thought that was going to happen. Enjoy your wedding, and I'll enjoy the fifty bucks I just made. Base out."

The line went dead.

Ben shook his head, struggling with a smile. "Laying it

on a little thick, weren't you?"

Nick pulled Ben to him. "What I said is true. You are the love of my life."

They heard the music start. Taking each other's hands, they proceeded through the door.

***

The ceremony was beautiful. Just as they kissed, a flock of birds erupted outside the plate glass windows behind the Justice of the Peace.

After a startled look out the window, Ben turned to Nick.

"That wasn't part of our ceremony, was it?" *Did Nick add it to the plan without telling me?*

His new husband shook his head. "Um, wasn't me. Those were doves. They're going to die in this heat."

"Then who…"

His mother stepped up beside them. "I thought it would be a nice touch. Isn't it traditional to release doves at a wedding?"

"Not in in the middle of the desert, Mom!" Ben protested. Reconsidering, he started again. "Um, thank you. I'm glad you came around and supported my decision. Even if you *did* wear black to my wedding."

His mother continued, oblivious to his sarcasm. "They were all I could find on short notice. Oh, and I got you

11

boys a present, too. I left it at your house."

Ben groaned inwardly. *The last present she got me was a Denebian Trangler. It took me weeks to get the damn thing off the ceiling of my apartment. Thankfully, when I suddenly hung several flags and blankets across my ceiling to 'make it feel like a Moroccan lounge', Nick didn't suspect anything.*

Hours later, after everyone else had left the reception, they finally made it home to find out what his mother had gotten for them.

Cautiously opening the front door, Ben peered inside.

"What are you expecting?" Nick asked from behind him.

"You never know with my mother," Ben said flatly.

A scrabbling sound caught their attention. They turned to see two balls of golden fur flying in their direction.

Nick scooped one up. "Puppies? She got us puppies?"

"Cocker spaniels from the looks of them."

His husband groaned. "What are we going to do with them?"

Ben smiled. "Keep them, of course." A sly smile crossed his lips. "I even know what we can name them. "Al and Lien"

Nick snorted. "Al-Lien. Cute." He rubbed the little dog's head. "Hello, Al."

Ben grabbed the other puppy off the floor. "I guess that makes you Lien then."

The puppy still in his arms, Ben grabbed Nick and pulled him into an embrace, giving him a deep kiss.

Unidentified Love

When he pulled back, he said, "Well, you've finally got your Al-Lien and you can come home to them and me every night."

Chapter Three

Ben stretched out, tensing every muscle in his body. *Wow, this mattress is so comfy. We've got to get one for our place.* The thought brought him up short. *Our place. I can't believe we're finally married. After all these years together, the country and the military finally came around so we could get legally married.*

He looked at the man still snoozing next to him. *Today's the day. I'm finally going to tell Nick the truth about me. About where I'm from and what I am.* He let out a quiet chuckle. *He's going to lose it when he finds out that those aliens he's spent his whole life looking for have been right under his nose the whole time.*

It's our honeymoon. We're in Paris, the city of romance, a place where we're both aliens. What better time to tell him.

Nick stirred, flinging one arm over Ben's chest.

"Good morning, love," Nick said around a yawn.

"Wakey, wakey. We've got a lot scheduled for today. We need to get moving if we're going to hit all the sights before dinner. I got us reservations at the fancy place we walked by last night."

"Can't we just stay in bed? I don't get many vacations and I'd just like to relax. With you." Nick reached out and pulled me in for a deep kiss.

"Hey, you were the one who came up with this itinerary, not me. Though I've always wanted to see the Louvre. The rest? They aren't as important to me as spending time with you." Ben began drawing hearts in Nick's chest hair.

Nick shuddered. "Stop that! It tickles."

Ben let a wicked smile play across his lips. "I wonder where else I can tickle you?" He reached down under the covers.

"That doesn't tickle." Nick let out a low moan. "But it definitely feels good."

A couple hours later, they finally managed to get out the door of their hotel room.

Glancing down the street, they saw the road had been cordoned off and a parade was passing by behind the blockade. The two men shared a confused look.

Ben pulled out his guidebook. "Today's Assumption day. It's a big Catholic holiday. Lots of parades and feasting."

"Feasting? That sounds great. I'm starving," Nick complained playfully. "Where do you want to go for lunch?"

"Well, we certainly can't go that way. Let's see what we can find the other direction."

I was practically skipping as we left the patisserie. Lunch had consisted of freshly-made turkey sandwiches and then chocolate mousse piled on top of cherry cheesecake for dessert.

"Let's go for a walk along the Seine." Nick patted his stomach. "I need to work off all those calories or I won't fit into my uniform when we get back home."

"Yeah, like that's even possible." Ben scrunched up his eyes. "You've never had any trouble keeping your six-pack. You're over forty and still have the body of a twenty-year-old. Whereas I," he gestured down at his body, "have to be careful of every bite I eat or I'll blow up like a balloon. It's not fair. Damn this weird metabolism of mine."

"Well, I love you no matter what you look like." Nick pulled him into a tight embrace.

As we walked along the waterfront we saw several men with fishing poles lining the banks of the Seine. Nick homed in on a rack of fishing poles but the sign above it in French baffled both of us. Our puzzlement brought first one, then two of the fishermen to our sides.

There was much gesturing from our new friends, as well as bits and pieces of English. "You fish?" He handed a cane pole to Nick. Pointing at the Seine, he said, "Everyone fish in shallows now. Is a festival. You catch, you eat." He mimed eating the fish.

Nick looked at me. "We already have dinner plans for tonight. Maybe we can catch something tomorrow and cook it ourselves for dinner?"

He glanced down at his watch, then looked up nervously. "Ummm...," he began.

Uh, oh. I know that look. It's the one Nick gives me whenever he knows what he's about to say will upset me.

"I sorta have a meeting I need to get to this afternoon." Nick gave him a toothy grin. "I was gonna duck out while we were in the Louvre, but we got such a late start..."

"Are you kidding me? What kind of meeting could you

16

have in Paris?" Realization dawned. "Wait. Was this whole trip because you had a meeting here, not just because I wanted to come here for our honeymoon?"

Nick shrugged. Sheepishly, he said, "Um, two birds, one stone?"

Ben crossed his arms. "This had better be good."

"I'm meeting with the head of the European Space Agency to discuss working together in our search for extraterrestrials. It shouldn't take long, that's why I planned on going while you were looking around the Louvre. I'm sure he wouldn't mind if you tag along. It's not like we're discussing any sensitive material."

Ben considered for a few minutes. *Extraterrestrials? Like me? This could be fun. Plus, it might be a good chance for me to find out what they know. That'll give me the perfect opening to discuss my...unusual origin over dinner tonight.*

"Okay, let's get it over with so we can spend a couple hours at the Louvre before dinner."

Nick pulled out his phone and summoned an Uber.

Twenty minutes later, they were signing in at the guard station at the ESA-HQ. The head of the agency, a large florid man in his sixties, met them once they were through security.

"Good afternoon, gentlemen. I am Lorenzo Arcuri

"I am excited to meet with the head of the American search for extraterrestrial life. Which one of you is General Pearson?"

Nick smiled and shook the man's hand. "I am, Signore

Arcuri."

"And you are his aide, yes?"

Ben shook the man's hand, his grip firmer than was absolutely necessary. "Aide? No, I'm his husband." He shot a look at Nick, daring the man to contradict him.

The Italian cleared his throat. "Ah, I see."

Nick stepped in front of me. "It's fine, Signore Arcuri. Ben knows what I do for a living. We've known each other all our lives. He's well aware of my obsession with all things extraterrestrial." He gestured toward me. "You can speak freely in front of him."

"Excellent. Please follow me. My office is just down the hall."

Once they were comfortable in the leather wing-back chairs, the ESA director launched into his spiel.

"We have never been able to get close to any of the craft that have entered our airspace. They easily outrun even our fastest jets."

Ben smiled inwardly. *Yeah, and you have a few hundred years worth of advancements before you can even come close to catching one of us.*

"But, we're developing a weapon we believe will be able to disable one of their ships so we can finally capture and study these aliens."

A weapon? I'm not sure I like the sound of that.

"What kind of weapon, sir?" Ben asked leaning forward. "If you don't mind me asking. I mean, if you can't even get close to them, what kind of weapon could affect them?"

"It is a combination rail gun and high-powered laser. We figure they probably have some kind of physical or energy shields, so we plan to overload both systems simultaneously to disrupt their power and bring the ship down. The UFO that buzzed across the Atlantic and your United States last month was what gave us the idea."

Damn, it would probably work too, Ben thought in dismay. *The feedback from both systems at once could knock the power out long enough for them to crash. Wait. Last month? That was mom showing off on the way to our wedding! I'll bet she hoped Nick would leave me at the altar to go investigate. Hah! Was she wrong. Wait till I get my hands on her....*

Nick was nodding along with Arcuri.

"That's a great idea. We have prototypes of both of those weapons. I'm sure we could have a working model in under six months. This is great news."

Speak for yourself, Nick!

"Yes, it is, General. And we've already built a secure facility where we can study and dissect these aliens once we have them in our custody. Just think of what we could learn from experimenting on them. We could find out their tolerances. Maybe even find some kind of biological weapon that we could use against them."

Holy supernovas. This guy's a maniac. He sounds like Josef Mengele. Wanting to dissect people and perform experiments on them. He turned to look at his partner. *And he's just sitting there nodding along like what the guy is suggesting wasn't insane.*

"Surely you can't be serious?" Ben said, squirming slightly in his chair. "You're talking about performing experiments and dissection on living beings."

"But they're not human, so there's nothing to worry about," the ESA director said with a dismissing wave of his hand. "It isn't like they haven't been kidnapping us for years and experimenting on us."

That's never happened, Ben thought with disgust. *It's all just a bunch of stupid stories told by hicks who got so blackout drunk they needed a convenient excuse.*

Ben was about to contradict the man when Nick put his hand over mine.

"We should probably stop here," Nick said, rising from his seat. "We have dinner reservations in an hour and we need to get back to our flat and get ready. We *are* on our honeymoon after all. Thank you for your time, Signore Arcuri. I'll be in touch to work out the details of our cooperation."

They stood and Nick shook hands with the ESA director, saying their goodbyes.

By the time they were outside on the street waiting for their Uber to arrive, Ben's thoughts were racing.

I don't dare tell him about me now. Not when he just sat there smiling and nodding while that psychopath said all those horrible things. Does he think like that, too? I know he loves me, but would he hand me over to these monsters if he knew the truth? I can't risk it. I can never tell Nick who I really am.

A lone tear slid down his cheek.

* * *
***

"General Pearson, how did your meeting with Arcuri go while you were in Paris?"

Nick looked up from the report he was filling out. His superior, General Adams, stood in the doorway to his office.

"Unbelievable, sir," he said, shaking his head. "I'm recommending that we not pursue this partnership with the ESA. Their director gave me the creeps." Nick slammed his pen down on the desk. "The man is deeply disturbed. I like their ideas about how to bring down an alien craft." He chuckled. "I've never hidden the fact that I want to meet an alien face-to-face, after all." He felt his pulse racing as he recounted his conversation with the director. "He was advocating dissecting the aliens, performing experiments on them. Not on ones who had died, but on living creatures. They already have a facility built to hold them and conduct these...atrocities. He sounded excited about building what to all intents and purposes is an alien Auschwitz."

Nick shuddered. Standing up, he braced his arms on the desk.

"Sir, as long as this is my command, I will *not* allow that to happen to any sentient being."

His boss thought for several moments, running his

hands around the brim of his hat.

"Well, I can see your point. If you feel that strongly about it, I'll convince the Joint Chiefs that this is a bad idea." He snickered. "I'll just tell them that it would be a huge PR nightmare if it ever got out that we sanctioned the creation of an Auschwitz-type facility."

"Thank you, sir."

After General Adams left, Nick sat down and leaned his head against the back of the chair. Closing his eyes, his thoughts turned to his husband.

Ben didn't seem to like Arcuri, either. I thought for a moment he was going to launch himself across the desk at the director. He's got such a big heart and he's so protective of others. That's one of the things I love most about him. An odd thought crossed his mind. *Hmmm. I wonder how Ben would react if he ever actually met an alien. Ha! Like that'll ever happen.*

Chapter Four

"Okay, I'll meet you at the ranger station for evac. Pearson out."

The look in his husband's eyes when he turned around almost made him call the chopper pilot back to cancel the evac. *Surely he'll understand. He knows how long I've been searching for extraterrestrial life. This might be my chance to finally prove they are real.*

"I'm sorry, honey. I know I promised that I wouldn't let anything interrupt our vacation this time, but the base picked up a UFO on the radar. I have to go back. I'm in charge of the search for ETs. If this really is aliens, it could change everything."

Ben shook his head and pinched his nose.

I know that look. Nick winced inwardly. *I'm in for it now.*

"Nick... You gave me your word; this time, no interruptions! We haven't had time away without the 'base,'" he made air quotes around the word, "needing you for something, in years. Hell, they even called during our damn wedding ceremony. I had to threaten to leave you just to get you to finish your vows. I'm sick of it." He stomped off a few paces. "You're not in a relationship with me, you're in a relationship with that, that base! You should have married it, not me."

Ben's shoulders slumped and he hung his head. "I love you, Nick. But I don't know if I can handle always being second in your life. Besides, isn't that what you left Miles in charge for? So he could handle anything that came up while we were on our vacation? Let him handle it. Stay here with me."

"Ben, I love you too, but," he said, trying and failing to pull his husband into a hug, "this is a big deal. I might finally be able to prove there are aliens here on this planet."

"That's not the point. The point is, you're breaking your promise. Again." The man's face could have been set in stone.

Nick shook his head. "I have to go. The chopper's on its way." Tilting his head and smiling, he asked, "Can I at least get a kiss goodbye?"

The other man sighed, a strange, wistful look on his face that Nick couldn't quite read. "Okay, one kiss. Goodbye, my love."

As he was leaving, he heard Ben take a call. "It looks like you were right, Mom. See you soon."

***

"What's the situation with the UFO?"

The lieutenant who met him at the door snapped a quick salute before matching strides with him and launching into his report.

"Sir, Flight Control has been tracking the unidentified object for nearly two hours now. It first showed up entering our atmosphere somewhere over the Atlantic Ocean, then began heading west. At one point, we thought it was coming directly toward the base, but just after we spoke, it changed course and now appears to be heading for southern California."

Maybe I should call Ben and tell him look outside. Maybe he can spot whatever this is. He chuckled to himself. *Wouldn't that be funny? I come all the way back to the base and he ends up with a front row seat for a real alien spacecraft.*

Walking into the command center, he took in the information displayed on the various monitors arrayed across one wall of the room.

"Jackson, am I reading that correctly? The craft has halted?"

"Yes, General Pearson. It's come to a stop over the southern end of the Sequoia National Forest.

Panic flooded Nick's heart. *That's where our cabin's at. Ben's there all alone.* Grabbing his phone, he hastily called his husband's cell. It rang and rang until the voicemail picked up. *Stop it. He's fine. He probably just has it on vibrate. Or he's still mad at me. Stop worrying.*

"Sir, the object just disappeared from radar."

"What? Where did it go?"

"I don't know, sir. One moment it was there, the next it was just gone."

"Miles, what happened to the jets that were dispatched to follow the object?"

"They never even got close to it. Every time they tried,

it either climbed above their ceiling or dropped so low they lost visual contact."

Nick let out a heavy sigh. "Jackson, contact the jets. Have them do a fly-by of its last known position. STAT!"

"Yes, sir!"

Nick paced the worn carpet, torn between worry that something might have happened to Ben and his commitment to the program. He'd been eager to find proof of ETs when he first got to Groom Lake, the famous Area 51, but now... Now more than anything, he just wanted to be back in his husband's arms.

One of the technicians let out a surprised yelp. "Sir! It's back!"

Nick's eyes flew to the monitors. Sure enough, he could see the tell-tale blip on the radar screen.

"What's it doing? It looks like it is just sitting still."

"No, sir. It's climbing. Straight up. At Mach 4!" The tech all but screamed the last three words. "It's gone. It's out of our atmosphere!"

"Can you tell where it's heading?"

Silence followed, then the tech shook his head. "We've lost it, sir. It's not showing up on any of our sensors."

The entire room seemed to hold its breath, waiting for the general to make a decision.

"Stand down." He waved to his second-in-command. "Miles, take over. Review everything we collected and have a report ready for me when I get back from my vacation. Right now, I need to get back to my husband."

Miles nodded, then lowered his voice. "Do you think Ben's ever going to forgive you for leaving in the middle of *another* vacation?"

Nick chewed his lip for a moment before answering. "I'm sure he will. He always does. But this has got to be the last time. He's the best thing that ever happened to me. I couldn't bear it if I lost him."

Miles slugged him in the shoulder. "About time you realized that. That man of yours is a real catch. If I bent that way, I know I wouldn't leave him alone for anything."

Nick nodded to his friend. "Hold down the fort. I'll be back on the thirtieth." As he left the command center, he called his helicopter pilot. "Jake, get the 'copter ready. I'm heading back to the cabin...."

***

"Honey, I'm home," Nick called into the dark cabin.

A quick check on his locator app showed that Ben was still out in the woods. Grabbing a jacket, he headed out to the clearing where they sometimes built bonfires and watched the stars. He followed their footprints from earlier in the day until he came across his husband's cell where it lay beside their tracks.

He scanned the area, his eyes anxiously searching for any sign of Ben.

Nothing.

Turning the cell phone on, he was surprised to hear his husband's favorite song spilling from the small speaker. Elvis Presley was softly crooning *As long as I have you.*

Tears welled up in Nick's eyes, so much so that it took him a minute to realize that there was also a message on the screen.

My dearest Nick,

I can't do this anymore. I'm tired of waiting for you to see what's right in front of you, instead of staring off at the stars. My mother warned me you'd break my hearts. Turns out she was right. I'm going home with her.

I'll always love you.

Ben

Looking up, he had just enough light from the setting sun to see the outline of a great circle scorched into the clearing. He let the night fall around him, staring up as each new star became visible.

The alien ship...Ben.... Realization washed over him in a cold wave.

Which one of those stars do you call home, my love?

Chapter Five

Dr. Elise Templeton was tapping her pen on the yellow pad in her lap.

"So you mentioned at the end of our last session that you've had recurring nightmares. Would you care to elaborate?"

Nick fidgeted in the plump, overstuffed chair.

"The dreams started," he paused a moment, "about four months ago. I'm in heaven, I think. There's a man with great sad eyes leading me around, showing me various sights. Then, for some reason, I pull a gun, put a muffler on it, and kill him." Nick shook his greying head, looking pleadingly at the doctor. "Why would I do that? In heaven of all places?"

She was slow to reply to him. Tapping her pen on her lip, he could almost hear the gears turning in her head.

"You know, it sounds like you're following St. Bernard. You know, from Dante? The one who shows him around heaven?"

Of course it would be from that. Ben's favorite. He fought back tears.

"Yes, Dr. Templeton, I'm familiar with the reference. But why would I kill him?"

"I think it has to do with Ben and your relationship. I see this sometimes in divorced military men." She chuckled. "Not the Dante reference, of course. Most men dream of killing the mailman. Now that's a thankless job."

Nick ran his fingers through his close-cropped hair.

"But what does it *mean*?"

Sobering, she said, "Well, my take on the dream is that you think you 'killed' the man who brought you to heaven. Ben. That it was your fault that you lost him." She pursed her lips. "I think that you have bigger issues than the low self-esteem you claimed was causing your erratic behavior."

He buried his head in his hands. "I always felt we were destined to be together." He looked up at her. "He's been in my life since we were kids. He was always the best part of me. Since he's been gone...I feel like half a man.

"Then don't give up on him," she said simply. *As though that would heal my broken heart.* "Go and find him and tell him how much you love him."

"If I only could, I would, but I can't. He's gone."

She raised an eyebrow at him. "You're telling me that with all your contacts and all the resources at your disposal, you can't find one man on this planet?"

He's probably not on this planet. Not after I drove him away. If only I'd put him first, not my work.

***

Nick drove home through the gathering dusk. Walking through their home, he stopped to feed Al and Lien, then let himself out onto the back porch. He sat alone, unmoving, as the sky darkened and the stars came out, pinpricks of light in the velvet of the sky.

The silence felt heavy. Ben had always talked his ear off about the stars when they sat out here. *Hell, he's probably visited them.*

Raising his face to the sky, he pleaded, "I'm sorry, Ben. Please come back. I need you."

Chapter Six

Nick tossed the pills into his mouth. Taking a swig from the bottle of whiskey on his desk, he washed them down.

"I hope those were just vitamins and not something medicinal," Miles said from the doorway. "I don't want to call 911. The paperwork I'd have to fill out if my boss committed suicide in his office would take me weeks." Turning serious, he asked, "Are you okay?"

Nick reached into the desk and pulled out the bottle of vitamins, shaking it at his friend. "I'm as okay as I can be, all things considered." Putting his elbows on the desk, he buried his face in his hands. "Who am I kidding? Nothing's been okay since Ben left." He put the vitamins away and pulled two glasses from the drawer. Pouring an inch of whiskey in each, he handed one to Miles.

"I hear congratulations are in order." He held up his glass in a toast. "I just received word that they are pulling my command and giving it to you. I told them they were making the right choice."

Miles nodded, making himself comfortable in the visitor's armchair. "I just heard too. That's why I came over here. Did they tell you why?"

"They feel I've been getting 'too erratic' over the last year. That I've 'lost my focus', whatever that means." He knocked back half the whiskey in one gulp. "Even my meetings with that shrink, Dr. Templeton, didn't help. I still can't sleep through the night. And my nightmares have only gotten worse."

Miles interrupted his downward spiral. "You've been working too hard. Spending every waking moment looking for Ben." He ran a hand through his sparse salt-and-pepper hair. "Maybe you just need to get away, relax for a bit. Hopefully, that will calm—"

"I've decided to leave the military." The words hung in the silence.

Snapping his mouth shut, Miles said, "That's a pretty big decision. Don't you think you should take some time? You've spent the better part of your life in the military, you wanna throw that all away? For what? Ben is gone." He gave a low throaty chuckle. "What are you going to do, just go disappear to that cabin with your mutts until you die?"

Nick shook his head. "For as long as I can remember, I've been obsessed with finding aliens. I was too focused on finding them out there," he pointed to the sky outside the window, "to realize I had one in my bed every night."

Miles had been about to take a drink of the whiskey when he abruptly set it back down on the desk. "Wait. You're telling me Ben was an alien? You're kidding, right?"

Nick let out a heavy sigh. "Nope. That UFO we spotted the day he disappeared? I found burn marks on the ground near our cabin and a goodbye message on his cell phone. I'm pretty sure the UFO was there to pick him up and take him home." He coughed a short laugh and rolled his eyes. "That explains a lot, too, like why his mom did all that weird stuff at our wedding. She probably didn't know any better."

Miles shrugged. "Or maybe she knew and just didn't approve of him marrying a human?"

"That's probably it then. That woman's hated me with a passion ever since we were kids."

The other man took a slow swallow of his whiskey. "Are you sure I can't change your mind? Get you to stay with the program?"

"It's too late." Nick downed the last of his whiskey. "I can't be here – be part of this program. This place doesn't hold anything for me anymore. It's taken me too long to realize that."

His best friend in all the world rose from his seat and stepping around the desk, pulled him into a bear hug.

"You do what you need to. Just take care of yourself. I'll handle things here." Stepping back, he shook a finger at Nick. "Just don't forget that you invited me to go fishing at your cabin. You haven't seen the last of me."

***

It had been several weeks since he'd said his goodbyes and moved back to the cabin. He'd spent every day since unpacking boxes. Every time he found something of Ben's, all work stopped as he held whatever it was and

34

cried. Tonight, he'd finally unpacked the last box. *Gods, I don't think I've ever hurt this much, physically and mentally. Not even boot camp was this agonizing.*

Walking down the hallway, he ordered the dogs out of the bedroom. "Sorry, guys, daddy's exhausted and needs a nice long soak in the tub to wash away all the hurt. I'll let you back in later. I don't want to sleep in that big empty bed all by myself either."

Lowering himself into the near-scalding water, he laid back and felt the tension in his muscles finally begin to loosen. He caught himself humming a tune he hadn't thought of in years.

He began to sing aloud.

Reunited. *Peaches and Herb. That's who did it. Ben and I sang that song one year with choir.* He closed his eyes. *Mr. Jones got so mad at us for passing notes in his classroom I thought sure he was going to throw us out.*

He kept singing the song, even as tears fled down his cheeks to join the bathwater. When he came to the chorus, he could've sworn he heard an echo. *I've never noticed an echo in here before. Even when Ben used to sing in the shower every morning.*

Coming to the chorus for a second time, he was positive he heard the echo. Bolting upright in the cooling water, he stopped singing. The echo finished the chorus without him.

Wrapping a towel around his waist, he burst into the bedroom.

He nearly collapsed at the sight before his eyes.

Ben was lying across the big bed, naked, save for some carefully placed red bows. One was tied around his neck. Another looked for all the world like a flag begging to be saluted.

It was only then that Nick realized the apparition was still singing.

He blinked and rubbed at his eyes. "Are you really here? Or have I finally lost my mind?"

Ben smiled in that radiant way Nick remembered. "Yes, love, I'm really here." He patted the bedspread next to him as he continued, "Your work was always more important than I was. You could have moved on after I left. Or taken some time off to get your head on straight and then gone back to it. But you didn't. You left. You gave it up of your own free will."

Nick leaned down over the edge of the bed, reaching out to touch his husband's face. *He's really here!*

"So I'm back." Ben looked at him, lust filling his gaze. He grabbed the towel around Nick's waist and pulled him down onto the bed.

"And I'm never letting you go again."

***

Several hours later, they disentangled themselves and sat up.

Nick wiped the sweat from his brow. "I need a shower. Wanna join me?" He shot a lewd look at Ben, still sprawled across the covers. "We can get cleaned up so we can get dirty all over again."

"In a minute. I still need to say 'hi' to Al and Lien. I've missed those little rascals," Ben said, watching his lover walk into the bathroom. When he heard the water start up, he hopped off the bed and opened the door. The two cocker spaniels bounded into the room. Sitting down on the side of the bed, he wrapped them up in a big hug.

Glancing at the bathroom door to be sure Nick was occupied, Ben dug his cell phone out of his folded pants on the chair. Dialing a number from memory, he waited until a groggy voice answered.

"Yeah?"

"Miles? It's Ben. I just wanted to tell you thanks for taking care of him while I was gone. And for letting me know that he had moved back into our cabin."

"You're there already?" Miles chuckled. "Wow, that was fast."

Ben snickered. "Mom drove. You know how she is. Anyway, I gotta go. He's waiting for me. Thanks again."

Miles' laughter came across the line. "Hey, that's what big brothers are for, right?"

Chapter Seven

"My condolences on your loss, Mrs. Pearson," Ben said quietly, wrapping his arms around the weeping woman.

"I can't believe he's gone. Dad was always so...larger than life." Nick shook his head. *I want to wrap my arms around her so bad, but HE always discouraged physical affection. 'Not manly,' he said. Like being human and feeling for others was a bad thing.*

"When I was a kid," Nick said, "he was this imposing general, larger than life and always barking out orders. Then I went into the military and lived constantly in his shadow. Every command I got stationed at knew him. 'Oh, you're Pearson's boy. You've got big shoes to fill, young man.' It took me forever to convince people that I actually knew what I was doing. Even then, I was just 'a chip off the old block,' like Dad was completely responsible for my success."

He let out a sigh. "I'm sorry, everyone. This all happened so fast. I'm still not thinking clearly."

Turning to the others still standing at the graveside, he tried to plaster a smile on his face, with only limited success. "I really appreciate you coming, Mr. and Mrs. Smith. I know it couldn't have been easy for you to get here on such short notice."

Ben's mom, Janet, placed a gloved hand on her son-in-law's arm. "Of course, Nicolas. We were coming to visit you boys when Ben messaged us that your father had passed, so we were already in the area."

Turning to Nick's mom, she continued, "I don't believe you've met my husband, Allen."

Ben's dad extended his hand. "Pleased to finally meet you, Mrs. Pearson."

Tears welled up in her eyes. "I've been just Mrs. Pearson, or 'the general's wife' for so long. Please, call me Melissa." She dabbed at the corners of her eyes with a handkerchief. "I've got nothing left to live for. I dedicated my whole life to that man and what do I have to show for it?"

Janet's perfect eyebrows shot up. "How can you say that? You've got a wonderful son." She smiled at Nick. "I'll admit, I was initially against this thing between Ben and Nicholas, but he's grown on me over the years." Looking Melissa right in the eyes, she said, "You should be proud. You've raised a good man."

Standing straighter, Melissa replied, "You're right. He is. I'm just, I don't know, feeling sorry for myself. I never got to live a life of my own." She looked around at the circle of faces. "I always did what I was supposed to do, which was seldom what I wanted to do." She took a deep breath and looked at Nick. "I know I shouldn't speak ill of the dead, but your father was not a nice man."

Nick sighed. *And don't I know it! He was the worst father, but I sure learned a lot from being his son.*

"I gotta admit, Dad pushed me a lot when I was younger, but I know he loved me." He placed a hand on his mother's shoulder. "He had such a big personality... It was like I couldn't breathe around him sometimes."

Her voice flat, Melissa muttered, "Try being married to him."

He watched her struggle to smile. "Did you know we were high school sweethearts? He decided that I was his sophomore year and that was that. He never let me make a decision for myself after that. Ever."

Tears began rolling down her cheeks. She swiped at them furiously before looking up into his face. "I tried to protect you. I did." She put her hand on top of Nick's. "Every time you didn't live up to what he thought you *should* be, he took it out on me." He saw his look of horror mirrored in her eyes.

Hastily, she amended her statement. "Oh, he never hit me, but honestly it might have been better if he had." She sniffed back more tears. "At least then I could have gone to someone for help. Said, 'Look at these bruises. See how he treats me?' Maybe someone could have helped me get away from him before I wasted my entire life."

Nick felt hot tears welling up in his own eyes for the first time that day.

"Mom? It was really that bad for you? Honestly, I never knew. I thought you were happy. I thought it was just me that couldn't handle living in his shadow."

His mom shook her head, casting her eyes to the ground. "And now," she said, holding out her wrinkled hands, "it's too late. I'm almost eighty-five. What kind of life do I have to look forward to? A nursing home?"

Nick's heart swelled up with love when Ben interjected, "You could come live with us. We'd love to have you."

She waved him off. "I couldn't. I refuse to be a burden on you boys."

Out of the corner of his eye, Nick saw his in-laws exchange a look. Tossing a glance at Ben, he silently mouthed, *What's up with them?*

Ben shrugged.

Janet took Allen's hand and held it to her cheek. The pair had identical inscrutable smiles across their faces.

"You know," Janet began, "it's not too late for you to have a life." She gestured around the cemetery. "What do you have left tying you to your old life, other than Nick, of course?"

His mom seemed to consider that for a moment. "Nothing." She gave a small shake of her head. "Isn't that pathetic? I wasn't allowed to have any friends of my own. I only socialized with people that worked with my husband in the military."

She fixed Ben's parents with a calculating look. "Why? Are you going to take me for a ride in your spaceship to see the universe before I die?"

The only sound that penetrated the ensuing silence was a lone bird calling from the nearby forest.

All eyes turned on Nick.

He quickly raised his hands. "Don't look at me. I didn't say anything."

Turning to his mother, he asked, "How did you...? When? I don't understand."

Eyes still bright from unshed tears, his mom shot him a sly grin.

"I wasn't sure until your wedding. Ben was always a little...different. Ever since you were kids. He reminded me of the foreign diplomats I met with your father over the years. Like he wasn't quite sure of himself in our culture. It stuck with me..."

"But how..."

She held up a finger to stop him. "Just a moment, I'm talking. When I heard the two of you arguing in the hallway at your wedding, I started to put it all together." She shook her finger at him. "Ever your father's son. You almost left your own wedding because of a UFO sighting."

Ben tried interrupting her this time. "Surely you don't believe..."

This time she chuckled. "Between your odd behavior when you were younger, the UFO sighting, Janet's black dress and those doves in the middle of the desert at the wedding? I just put it all together." Nick's mom tilted her head at him. "That must have been some conversation, when you told Nick you were an alien."

Ben scrunched up his face. "Ummm. Actually, I didn't tell him. At least not for a while. Nick didn't find out until that year we were separated. He figured it out on his own then."

She turned to look at Nick, her eyebrows rising. "You didn't know? For all those years?" The woman began to chuckle. "I can't believe *I* figured it out before you did. And you're the expert on aliens."

That got everyone laughing.

"But you, young man," she said, looking sideways at Ben. "I'm sure you had your reasons for not telling him. Lord knows he can be thick at times. Too much of his father in him." She sighed heavily. "At least you were finally honest with each other."

Turning to address Ben's parents, she returned to her original line of questioning. "So, am I right? Are you going to take me out there," She waved a hand toward the sky. "to see the universe?"

Ben's mother coughed. "Well, we were planning to invite the boys to come off planet with us in a few years." She reached out and pulled his mom into a hug. "We weren't going to offer to take them away while you were still alive. We couldn't take Nicolas from you like that. But," she said, gesturing toward the woods beyond the cemetery's gate, "if you come with us....?"

It didn't take long for his mom to decide. Nodding, she said, "I've always loved looking up at the stars. I think I'd like to see them up close."

Ben glanced between his parents. "Mom, Dad? You were really going to offer to take us? Both of us? I figured you'd wait until Nick passed away before you let me come home."

Janet and Allen both laughed.

"No, my darling. I may not have approved at first, but I can see how much you two love each other." She nodded at Ben. "And you proved me wrong. He didn't break your hearts. And your brother has told me repeatedly what a good man he is."

Nick swiveled to look at Ben. "Your brother?"

Ben scrunched his eyes shut. Opening one eye, he spit out, "Miles. He's my big brother."

What? Miles! All this time...

Nick's voice cracked. "I turned the American military's search for extraterrestrial life over to an alien." His eyes were tearing up. "Oh my god, that's priceless."

Drawing attention back to herself, Nick's mom asked eagerly, "So when do we leave? I'd like to see the universe before I die. I ain't getting any younger, after all."

Allen, quiet till now, smiled down at her.

"We can leave right now, if you'd like."

Her eyes went wide. Sputtering, she said, "But I need to take care of things. Sell the house. The car. Deal with life insurance...."

Allen waved her concerns away. "Don't worry about those things. We have people who can take care of all that for you." He turned to Ben and Nick. "How about it, boys? Are you ready to come with us too?"

Still reeling from the revelation, Nick asked, "How many of you are there on Earth? You have 'people' who can take care of our stuff?"

Ben pulled him into a tight embrace. "We've been watching your planet for some time now. There are more of us here than you'd imagine. If mom and dad say they can get our things to us, then they can." Pulling back and taking Nick's hand, Ben asked, "What do you say? Wanna see the universe with me?"

Nick didn't hesitate for a second. "Of course. I'd go to the ends of the universe as long as I get to be with you."

Allen smiled at them all. "This way then."

He led them toward the nearby forest. Once they are out of sight of the road, he pushed a button on what looked like an ordinary cell phone.

The next thing Nick knew, they were standing on what could only be the bridge of an alien spacecraft. On one wall, a monitor showed the graveyard they'd just left.

This ship had to have been here all along, cloaked from view.

Janet scratched at her shoulder. "Excuse me for a moment. I've got to get this stuff off me. It itches."

Without another word, Janet crossed the room, stepping into an empty tube. The door whooshed shut behind her.

Nick's mother looked at Ben. "You do look human, right? She's not going to come out of there looking like something from a bad sci-fi movie is she?"

Ben's laughter filled the room. "No, nothing like that. We're very similar to humans on the outside, though our internal organs are a little different. Honestly, we're more alike than not."

Seconds later, the tube whooshed open again. Ben's mom stepped out, looking exactly like she had at their wedding over twenty years prior.

"I swear, that stuff is gross." She scrubbed a hand along the side of her face. "It *still* itches."

Allen stepped up to his wife, planting a kiss on the recently scrubbed cheek. "You look lovely as always, my dear." Continuing across the room, he sang out, "My turn!"

While the man went through his transformation, Ben explained, "My people live considerably longer than you humans do, so, in order to blend in, we make ourselves look older." He winked at Nick. "I've been doing it slowly to match you over the years."

After his father exited the tube looking as though he was in his early thirties, Ben took his turn.

Nick shuffled his feet, suddenly nervous.

The door opened.

Ben stepped out, looking exactly like he had when they graduated from college.

Nick let out a wolf whistle. "Wow. Sexy as ever. I can't wait to…" He looked down at his sixty-seven-year-old body. "The mind is willing, but the flesh is weak."

Ben held a finger up to Nick's lips. "Shush you. We'll be fine."

Janet took Nick's mom's hand. "Melissa, dear, the trip to our planet will take a while. It would probably be best if you rested. We don't want anything to happen before we get there."

Nick's mom protested. "But I want to see the universe, not sleep through it."

Janet patted her hand. "Don't worry, you will. Trust me, this is for the best." She helped the older woman into a different tube and touched a panel on the wall next to it. The door slid shut.

Ben took Nick's hand. "And as much as I'd like to spend the time with you, you should go into suspended animation too."

Nick stepped into the tube next to the one containing his mother. Ben leaned in and kissed him. "We'll be there before you know it. Dream about me and our new life together. I love you."

The door slid shut, plunging him into darkness.

***

Light dazzled his eyes. Blinking rapidly, the world swam into focus for Nick. He felt a firm hand clasp his arm. Eyes following the arm upwards, he found Ben smiling down at him.

"How are you feeling, my love?" Ben asked, his voice laced with concern. "I always have dry mouth after being in suspended animation," he said, handing Nick a bottle of water, "so I thought you might want this,"

Nick grabbed the bottle, opened it, and downed it in

one gulp.

"Thanks, I needed that." Stepping out of the chamber, he nearly fell.

"Whoa, there," Ben said, catching him. "You've been out for a while. Take it easy for a few minutes. Let your body adjust."

Nick blinked several times then shook his head. "I feel so weird. Like I've forgotten how to walk or something."

Ben let out a short chuckle. "Well, the gravity *is* a bit less than Earth normal. You'll get used to it after a while."

Nick looked his husband up and down, savoring the sight of his trim, youthful body. "It's going to take me a while to get used to seeing you in skin-tight clothing. You're going to give this old man a heart attack." He let out low whistle.

"What's this thing?" He poked at the touchscreen-like belt his mate was wearing.

"Don't do that!" Ben shouted, jumping backwards and batting his hand away. "Do you want us to crash into something?"

Eyes wide, Nick said, "Sorry, it looked cool. I didn't realize it controlled the ship."

Ben gave him a teasing look. "It doesn't. But you have to be careful what you touch around here. If you *do* touch the wrong thing, it really *could* cause us to crash."

"Okay, point taken." Peering around the bridge, he asked, "So, are we there yet? At your planet, I mean. It feels like it's only been a couple minutes since I went into that thing, but I'm guessing it's been a while."

"Right you are. It's been about a year and a half Earth time since you went to sleep."

"A year and a half! Holy shit. Blink and you miss everything around here."

Ben poked him in the shoulder. "I didn't want to wake you. I figured you needed your beauty sleep."

"Hey! You calling me ugly?" Nick frowned. "I may be old and wrinkly, but I'm not ugly."

For some reason he couldn't understand, that set Ben to laughing.

Nick shook his head. "Whatever. So, what did I miss?"

Stepping toward the next pod, Ben said over his shoulder, "Nothing much. It's been pretty boring actually." Opening the door, he reached inside, pulling out an attractive young woman who appeared to Nick's eyes to be in her late twenties.

Panic crept into Nick's voice. "Who's that? What happened to my mom?"

"Nicky?!" the woman said hesitantly.

Ice water raced through his veins. "Mom? But how...?"

She raised a tentative hand to his cheek, like she'd done ever since he was a kid.

She abruptly snatched it back, staring at her hand in something close to shock.

Nick looked at Ben questioningly. Ben smiled at him

like a Cheshire cat. Tapping his touchscreen belt, a reflective surface appeared in the air in front of Nick and his mom.

"Is that us, Nicky?" she said with wonder.

His voice quavering a bit, Nick said, "I think it is, Mom."

Ben's hand came to rest on Nick's shoulder as he explained.

"My people learned centuries ago that cells have a sort of internal clock that controls aging. It didn't take us very long to learn how to reset the clock. That's why we look the way we do. When I realized my mom was regressing your mother, I knew she'd let me regress you too." He placed an arm around Nick, giving him a quick hug. "The process of de-aging someone isn't instant, so it made sense to put you both in suspended animation during the procedure."

Keeping his hold on Nick, Ben turned to focus on Nick's mom.

"Melissa," he said quietly, "now you get that chance at a new life. On our world, you'll have around three hundred more years to explore before you need to worry about your life being over."

While his mother absorbed that, Nick turned to Ben with his own burning question.

"Does this mean *we* have three hundred years to look forward to being together?"

Ben sucked in his lip before answering.

"No, my love. Because you were younger than your mother when we reset your cells, we'll probably only have...five hundred years or so together." His smile broke like dawn across his face.

Nick sucked in a breath. *Five hundred years? That still isn't long enough, but it's a good start.*

Glancing out the viewport, he saw a spiral of moons circling a giant golden planet.

Ben came up behind him, resting his chin on Nick's shoulder.

"Welcome home, my love. We're starting over, but this time," he said, poking Nick in the ribs, "*you* get to be the alien."

About Kyros

Kyros has always been an avid reader and has
written short stories since he was in middle
school. In addition to writing, he's worked as an
EMT, a factory worker, a network engineer, and
an electrician in the military. Then in his late
30s, he went back to school to finish his degree.
He graduated in 2008 from the University of
Washington with a Bachelor's Degree in
Technical Communication. Even though he
worked in the software industry for a few years
writing help documentation, he never gave up on
his first love, writing fiction. When his job
abruptly endedin early 2013, he decided to try
his hand at finally writing the novel that had
been banging around in his head for at least
twenty years.

* * *

Like his co-author, Kyros grew up in a small town in Indiana in the middle of nowhere. As soon as he could, he left Indiana and headed west. This landed him in the Seattle area where he lived for eighteen years. Shortly after moving there he met his future co-author at a science-fiction convention. They became fast friends and even owned a bookstore together for a few years. Eventually work and his heart led him to the San Francisco Bay area where he currently resides with his two husbands, two dogs, and a very opinionated African Grey parrot named Abby.

About Orion

Orion has published short stories, poetry, and some non-fiction pieces, as well as a previous novel. Writing her first novel, a fanfic in the world of Blake's Seven, titled *Thieves in Time*, meant hauling her computer across two counties every weekend in the early nineties while working with her previous co-author. Some of her flash fiction can be seen in Wild Words, a collection of prompt-driven, five hundred word short fiction written by the members of the Kickstart Writers Meetup Group in Snohomish, WA. Dreaming of Xeres is the first book written

in the world of The Third War. She really enjoys
writing online with Kyros.

Orion has been a school teacher, librarian,
factory worker, office worker, jewelry maker,
glass etcher, gypsy business owner, science
fiction convention and SCA vendor,
metaphysical bookstore owner, and one summer,
a mail carrier for the railroad. Raised on a farm
in Indiana, she visited Europe at seventeen and
has lived in Illinois, two separate times in
California, and Hawaii. Currently, she resides in
Everett, WA with her two cats, a piano, and
walls lined with books. Her friends have sworn
that they'll never help her move again!

Free Preview of Dreaming of Xeres

Chapter 1

"Three…two…one."

Tessa cracked open her eyes, dark lashes veiling her expression from Riley. Sitting up slowly, she took a deep breath and stretched.

"How do you feel?" he asked, struggling to keep his voice calm. With any of his other clients, this would be easy. This client, and what she'd revealed, made his insides roil with questions. He forced himself to stay professional, at least until his subject was back in the here-and-now, not the there-and-then.

"Wonderful!" his subject said. "Like I've just had a nap."

"And do you remember any dreams you might have had during your nap?" he probed.

She frowned, her eyes unfocusing. After a moment, she shook her head.

"No, nothing." She looked up at him from the worn sofa they'd found and brought home to their third floor walk-up. It had taken several friends to horse it up the two flights of stairs, almost flattening Alex at the second bend. "That's good, right?"

Riley smiled down at her. "Yes, that's good," he assured her. Then he frowned. "I do have some questions, though, if you don't mind."

"About what?"

He tried to act nonchalant. "Oh, just some

background. That's all."

"Background, huh?" She raised a lone eyebrow at him and swung her legs over the side of the couch. Stretching one arm along the back cushions, she cocked her head at him. "Go for it, Doc Mezmer."

He smiled. She'd given him that name when they'd first met in college. *Maybe this won't be so bad,* he thought.

"Okay. First, have you been playing any new online games? One set on an alien planet, perhaps?"

She considered for a moment, then shook her head. "Nope. There *is* a new one I'd like to get my hands on, but it won't be out for a couple of weeks yet."

Riley sighed. *So much for that idea.*

"Uh, have you ever written a story about an alien planet?"

"Hmmm." He could see her consulting her inner filing cabinet. "I did make up a world of sparkly unicorns in the fourth grade. They could make cookies out of leaves and change water into lemonade. Does that count?"

He snorted a laugh. "No, but thanks for the visual." Turning serious, he continued, "Did that world have silver grass and trees with orange bark and blue leaves?"

Tessa's eyes widened and she went still. After a moment, she asked, her voice laced with tension, "Where did you come up with that image? I dreamt of that place a lot when I was little. It had turquoise waterfalls and the clouds were somewhere between gold and pink. The sun seemed smaller than normal, too." She paused, shaking her head. "I hadn't thought of it in years. Until recently. Those dreams started up again a few weeks ago." Her brow furrowed and she looked at him suspiciously. "How could you know about that? Am I talking in my sleep? Or have you been rummaging around in my brain during regressions?"

Riley reared back. "Who, me? That's not ethical and you know it!"

"Then where did you get it from?"

Riley inhaled deeply, steadying himself for whatever happened next. Taking her hand, he plunged ahead.

"I got it from your regression. Not just this one, but several of the previous ones too." He paused, letting her absorb that. He'd regressed her several times since he'd finished his hypnotherapy internship. He needed the practice and she was a willing and handy subject. It wasn't until he tried to delve into past lives that this unfamiliar world had begun to manifest. He'd tried to make sense of it, turning the information around and around, examining it like a gemstone cut in a novel way. No matter how he looked at it though, he couldn't find any explanation that made sense.

"And just now, you gave me more information that I hadn't gotten through the regressions." He paused, thinking about his next move. "Are there other details you can remember from that world? Scenery, people, anything?"

Tessa looked down at their joined hands. "Details?

Hmmm."

She looked up, meeting his gaze. Her face reddened slightly before she continued. "You're going to think I'm crazy."

Riley smiled at her. "Honey, I love you. I don't think you're crazy. But I *would* like to know more about this world you've dreamed of."

"Well, if you're sure. Let's see. The people there are shorter and more muscular, for a start."

Riley nodded. "Okay, so the gravity is heavier than ours. Good, good. Go on."

With a sigh, she dropped his hand and squirmed into a more comfortable position. She curled her legs under her and leaned her dark head against the heavy fabric of the sofa. Riley watched as her face lost its frown and took on a rather dreamy expression.

"I dreamt I had a kurvan named Jesler. I remember a small warm orange sun in a blue-green sky with fluffy honey-pink clouds. The trees are orange with blue leaves."

"Wait a minute, what's a kurvan?"

Tessa smiled, "You'd call it a pony."

He glanced down at his session recorder. *Good, it's still on.* At least he'd have something concrete to show his mentor, Dr. Jake Adams, when he saw him at the hypnotherapy convention in Seattle next weekend.

Tessa blinked and sat up straight. "Now, where did all that come from? Growing up, I soooo wanted a pony."

"Like you don't want a pony now," he scoffed. "If I have to watch another rerun of The Black Stallion, I'm gonna scream."

She smirked at him. "I only watch that when I'm really stressed. It's only been—"

"Let's see, six times this year? And it's only March!"

"It hasn't been that many."

"Trust me. I've counted."

She grinned sheepishly. "Well, business *has* been a little hectic lately. Diana and I finished our last project just under the wire. Okay, the client was extremely impressed and we *did* get a bonus, but stress is stress."

"And speaking of Diana, while you and Alex are away at the convention, we're having a spa day. If, that is, she can get away from her husband. I swear, if Bryce weren't so darn good looking, I'd tell her to ditch him."

"He's possessive?"

"Oh, yeah. She told me they got into fight after BayCon. Remember that picture of her getting hugged by some costumed Klingon? When Bryce saw that picture, evidently he flipped out. Demanded to know who she was having an affair with at the convention." Tessa laughed. "She told him, 'What? You think I'm having an affair? The only person I've ever slept with besides you is Tessa. And before you ask, we *just slept.*' As you can imagine, that didn't go over very well. She said it took a week before he stopped grilling her about it."

Looking Riley in the eye, she asked, "What if it'd been

me in that picture? Huh?"

Riley wrinkled his brow and shrugged. "I'd have figured he was from the Klingon Embassy and had had too many prune juices. You know how they are. Mostly harmless, despite their looks."

"See? No big deal." She sighed and stood up, stretching her arms over her head and rolling her shoulders. She paused. "Well, to give the guy the benefit of the doubt, he's never been to a science fiction convention, ever. Maybe he'd mellow out if he could tear himself away for a weekend in Never Never Land."

Riley had to agree. *Most people don't understand the sci-fi convention subculture. People seen in normal society as nerdy, flourish when surrounded by 'their people.'*

"I suppose," Riley said, shutting off the recorder. He stood and threw his arms about Tessa, impulsively kissing her on the nose.

"Gotta run, Tess. Still have some packing to do for *my* convention."

She laughed. "Well, it wouldn't do if the eminent Dr. Riley MacPherson, Clinical Hypnotherapist and Doctor of Psychology," She made air quotes around his name and titles. "was late for anything, now, would it?"

He sighed. *I never have to worry about getting an overinflated ego with her around. She'll always be there to pop my bubble if it gets too big.*

He shot her an affronted look, but that only caused her to giggle. Pulling her closer, he kissed her properly. After a few breathless moments, he stepped back and cocked his head. "Gonna miss me while I'm gone?"

"Not a bit," she said with an impish look in her eye. "After the spa, I might just laze about the house watching horse movies and eating bonbons."

He smirked. "Bonbons?"

***

Mezmer Notes - Update 12:

Subject Alpha still has no memory of the strange environment described during our regression sessions.

Information related in the most recent session:
- *Trees with orange bark and blue leaves*
- *Silver grass*
- *People are short and muscular (higher gravity perhaps?)*
- *Small orange sun*
- *Blue-green sky*
- *Fluffy pinkish-gold clouds*
- *Subject had a kurvan, a "pony-like" pet, named Jesler*

Information from previous sessions:
- *Turquoise water*
- *Pale orange ground*
- *Orange squirrel-like creatures*
- *Blue fruit that tastes like a mix of strawberry and mango (that the Subject didn't like and was being forced to eat)*

- *Bright red clothing (Subject could not explain what the clothing looked like)*

The level of detail that the Subject provides in our regression sessions amazes me. It's obvious they feel they are physically there in that place. But these details must be some made-up fantasy that the Subject is creating in their own mind. Other than the few questions after this regression, I have not discussed this with the Subject for fear of creating false memories or causing the Subject to make up details simply to please me.

I plan to discuss this case with Jake at the conference this weekend. Hopefully he can provide some insight into this strange 'world,' for lack of a better term. Maybe he's encountered something like this before and can advise me how to proceed. I haven't seen any other indications that the Subject possesses mental issues as might be indicated by the fabrication of an entire world like this.

Saving…

Chapter 2

Alex slid into the vacant seat next to Riley. Opening ceremonies were well underway in the ballroom. There were so many men and women in dark suits, Alex had the fleeting suspicion that he'd gotten the wrong conference, one for *Men in Black*.

"About time you got here," Riley hissed.

"Sorry. My plane was late and the bus from the airport was standing room only." Tapping Riley's arm, Alex asked, "How'd the workshop go?"

Riley replied, keeping his voice low, "Not sure. We'll talk later."

Alex settled back in the cushioned chair, trying to pay attention as prominent hypnotherapists were introduced, said a few words, then sat down. He grimaced. *Ye gods, this is enough to put anyone to sleep.* Fidgeting, he noticed several annoyed glances from both Riley and the man sitting on his other side.

A presence on stage caught his eye. Sitting up straighter, Alex focused as a Dr. Matthew Cadwallader was introduced. Though not particularly tall, the man exuded an aura that intrigued Alex. From his charcoal grey pin-stripe suit and black tie to his silvery hair and piercing blue eyes, the man radiated self-confidence and trust-worthiness. And he was fit, really fit.

"Who's he?" Alex whispered.

Riley turned, frowning. "That's the presenter who ran

the workshop I took before the conference. We'll be seeing a lot of him this weekend. "

"Huh. He seems…intriguing."

"Well," Riley said sourly, "you'll certainly get a chance to meet him. Besides having a table in the vendors room to promote his new book, he's also all over the program schedule. I doubt he'll have time to sleep."

The emcee wrapped things up and dismissed them. Around the room, people gathered up their belongings and filed out.

"Come on, Alex. I've got two panels before lunch. Then you and I are meeting Jake Adams for lunch."

The younger man nodded. "I've been looking forward to meeting him. From what you've said, he really knows his stuff." Smiling devilishly, he said, "I'd like to run some of my pet theories past him too."

Riley rolled his eyes. "No, not that. I have no idea *where* you get half your ideas."

"On the internet, of course," he replied. "Even something like my government hypnosis theory is worth considering, if only for a laugh."

"Right. We'll see whether Jake'll laugh at that one. I'm heading to my panel." He pulled out his schedule. "Life Between Lives: Filling Out the Forms." He looked up and grinned at Alex. "Sounds like fun, huh?"

Consulting his own pocket schedule, Alex countered with, "I have Interactive Sleep Hypnosis. I wonder if they'll provide pillows?"

Riley huffed a laugh and waved as he moved off. "Meet you at the hotel cafe at noon."

After his panels, Alex hurried to meet Riley. Spotting him from the cafe door, he quickly threaded his way through the crowded tables. He noticed Dr. Cadwallader holding court in a corner booth. The whole group seemed to be hanging on his every word. Alex pursed his lips and thought, *Man, that Cadwallader guy's charismatic, but there's just something...oily about the man. He's treating those people like they should be honored to worship at his feet.*

Coming up behind Riley, Alex saw he was in deep discussion with an older man. *So this is Riley's mentor, Jake. Damn. He's like a teddy bear done in silver and smiles. I bet his clients feel really comfortable talking to him.*

Riley looked up when Alex got to the table. Introductions were made while the waitress took their orders.

When she'd gone, Riley resumed his conversation with Jake. "I don't quite know what to think about the workshop I took from Cadwallader," he said, casting an eye at the crowd around the man. "His theories sound good, but...." He covered his face with his hand, then lowered his voice. "He raises the hairs on the back of my neck, Jake."

"Oh," said the big man, "so he gets to you, too."

Riley started. "You mean—"

Jake huffed. "Yeah. I've seen him around, sat in on a couple of his panels, read some of his theories online. I get the feeling there's something behind the façade, something I might not like. I can't quite put a finger on it though."

"Also, there was something odd that happened in that workshop." Riley paused, staring down at the white tablecloth for a moment. Looking up, he continued, "One of the therapists said, 'Next thing you know, everyone will be telling us about a world with orange-colored trees with blue leaves.' Weird, huh?"

Alex saw Riley holding his breath, waiting for...what? Alex didn't know.

Jake's eyebrows rose. "Orange trees and blue leaves?" the man sputtered. "Someone *else* mentioned that in a regression?"

Riley's eyes widened. He let out his breath in a rush. "You...you've heard that too?"

The man nodded, reaching for his water glass and taking a sip. "Twice. A thirteen-year-old abuse victim and a sixty-eight-year-old PTSD patient with chronic nightmares." He turned a querying look upon his protege. "You?"

"Once, so far. A twenty-eight-year-old woman."

Alex sat up straighter in his chair at the mention of Riley's client. *Wait, Riley doesn't have any clients that age. But isn't that how old Tessa is? I know she's asked Riley for a past life regression before. Still, what do orange trees and blue leaves have to do with her?*

"Four cases? That sounds like some kind of conspiracy

to me," Alex said with a grin.

Riley threw him a sour look, then returned his attention to the older man. "Anyway, Jake, I wondered if you would ask around at the conference. See if any other therapists are getting these same odd descriptions. I have a few meetings set up for this weekend, I'll ask them too."

Jake gave Riley a sharp look. "What are you thinking?"

"Right now, I really don't know. I need more evidence, more cases to work with." Riley caught first Alex's, then Jake's eyes. "Don't let anyone else know about our four cases, okay? I don't want to start a rumor or give anyone ideas or...or anything. Or," he said, glancing sharply at Alex, "start any wild ass conspiracy theories."

Alex gave Riley a 'Who, me?' look as both men nodded.

Their meals arrived, tabling further conversation on the subject.

***

Alex sat on the edge of his bed watching Riley crawl around on the floor trying to plug in his laptop.

Backing out from under the desk, Riley banged his head, grousing, "Is this room intentionally badly lit?" Twisting around, he ended in a cross-legged position on the beige carpet, looking up at Alex's knees.

Alex rose. "Need a hand up?" he asked, smiling.

"Sure."

Alex hauled him upright and suddenly found himself

70

nose to nose with his friend. For some reason, the man seemed a little out of breath.

"Wow, Alex, I didn't know you were that strong."

Alex contemplated the linked arms between their chests.

"There are a lot of things you don't know about me, Riley."

Staring into Alex's eyes, Riley asked, "Like what?"

Alex didn't speak for a moment, pondering his answer. *Is now the right time? I've been hoping for a chance. Maybe now is the right time.* Taking a deep breath, he plunged ahead.

"I'm bisexual."

The words hung in the air between them and the silence became almost tangible before Riley replied, "So?"

"I've been attracted to you ever since you saved me from getting crushed by that monster couch. I wondered...."

Alex left his words hanging. *He's not saying anything. He's disgusted. He's never going to speak to me again. Oh shit, why did I have to open my big mouth.*

Riley's eyes widened as the implications sank in. "You mean...you and me?" He gestured, indicating the two of them.

Alex could only nod. His tongue refused to participate.

Riley's lips quirked up in a wry twist. "I don't think that would be such a good idea, Alex. I'm supposed to be your mentor, your teacher. I'd feel like I was taking advantage of you." A lopsided grin broke over his face. "Not that I'm not flattered, mind you. If circumstances were different? Well, who knows."

Abruptly self-conscious about their linked hands, Alex pulled away. Riley, suddenly lacking Alex's support, stumbled, and plopped down heavily on the desk chair.

Alex gasped. "Are you okay?" He could feel the heat in his cheeks and his ears seemed to be on fire. Reaching out, he laid a hand on Riley's shoulder.

Riley looked up at him and nodded. "I'm fine." He turned to plug the power cord into his laptop, causing Alex's hand to slide from his shoulder.

Did he do that on purpose? I hope he doesn't feel uncomfortable around me now. Maybe I should ask....

Riley glanced over his shoulder. "I have to get these notes downloaded before I can get some sleep. My first panel tomorrow starts at nine. If I don't get some breakfast before that, I'll be nodding off all day."

Seeing Riley busy with his computer, Alex grabbed his toiletries bag and fled to the bathroom. Closing the door, he put his back to it and slid down to the aqua-tiled floor. Lacing his fingers behind his head, he brought his elbows in around his bowed head.

Crap! Well, at least that went better than I thought it would. Maybe after this mentoring thing is over.

***

Mezmer Notes - Update 15
National Hypnotherapy Conference in Seattle:

 The pre-con workshop was interesting, but the facilitator, Dr. Cadwallader, seemed more interested in pushing his new book than he was in actually teaching anything or answering any questions. However, I had some good conversations with the other participants, which made up for the lack of information in the actual workshop. The most surprising thing was something mentioned by a Dr. Thompson. He has a client who described trees with orange bark and blue leaves, exactly like Subject Alpha. When I questioned him further, I found other similarities between his patient's descriptions and those of Subject Alpha. He even offered to help with my research. I gave him one of my cards, and he promised to send me excerpts from his notes, minus any personal information, of course.

 Over lunch with Jake and Alex, I mentioned my conversation with Dr. Thompson. I was surprised that Jake had also encountered this before, in two separate cases: a thirteen-year-old abuse victim and a sixty-eight-year-old PTSD patient with chronic nightmares . That makes four unrelated cases of orange trees with blue leaves that I have discovered. I was curious when Subject Alpha described this strange landscape, but now I am eager to find if there are even more cases. How can these widely divergent people all be describing the exact same thing? Especially about something that doesn't exist.

 On a personal note, I'm a little flabbergasted that Alex told me he's attracted to me. I had no clue. I am a little concerned about how this might affect our working relationship. I rely on his assistance and really like him, but don't want to send the wrong message. If he wasn't my intern and I wasn't with Tessa, I might have taken him up on his offer. He's really sexy and handsome, but I love Tessa. Still, it's tempting.

Saving…

For the rest of the story, go to
https://www.amazon.com/dp/0996266518/